D0607177

FRECKLES

The Mystery of the Little White Dog in the Desert

What people are saying about *Freckles*

"A beautiful metaphor of nurturing and healing for children of all ages."

—Connie Carnes, Executive Director
The National Children's Advocacy Center
Huntsville, Alabama

"*Freckles* is a delightful book that captures your attention from the first page and keeps it. Not only is it fun to read, but woven throughout are important lessons about protecting family, being good friends, and how we can be of service to others. Entertaining, educational, and passionately written. I highly recommend this book!"

—Marty Becker, DVM, author of *The Healing Power of Pets*, co-author of *Chicken Soup for the Cat and Dog Lover's Soul* and *Chicken Soup for the Pet Lover's Soul*, and veterinary contributor to ABC-TV's *Good Morning America* and Walt Disney Television's Animal Planet series *Petsburgh, U.S.A.*, Twin Falls, Idaho

"Children who have crossed the desert land of abuse will find a soul mate in *Freckles*, both as a fellow survivor and as a source of comfort and understanding. This is a rich resource for therapists and programs dealing with children with a background of trauma."

—Holly Smart, Licensed Psychologist/Senior Therapist
Chrysalis Center for Women & Their Families
Minneapolis, Minnesota

"At ARF, our motto is *People Rescuing Animals—Animals Rescuing People*. Paul Howey's story about Freckles reflects the truth in that statement and shows that when animals and kids get together, magical things can happen. It is my hope that people young and old will read this heartwarming book and then choose to do something to make the world a better place for our children and for our animals."

—Tony LaRussa, manager of the St. Louis Cardinals, 4-time National League Manager of the Year, and founder of the Animal Rescue Foundation (ARF)
Walnut Creek, California

"A wonderful story—adventurous, educational, and loving with a touch of humor."

"The lessons of unconditional love between people, between animals, and between people and animals will stir the hearts of those who read this delightful and touching story."

"Freckles is one lucky dog. Readers will discover that those who experience and nurture a dog's ability to bring out the best in us are indeed among the blessed."

"This is one remarkable story. The therapeutic benefits of contact with companion animals…is slowly but surely becoming recognized by health care professionals throughout the world. It's always nice to be reminded of what our pets can do for us in such an enjoyable form as Freckles' story."

"A very moving story. We can think of no better way to teach children about responsible pet ownership than to weave the message into such a delightful children's book."

"Freckles' story is a testament to the will and determination mothers (whether two- or four-legged) in protecting their young. I am also pleased that the story stresses the importance of rescuing from a shelter and of obedience training. Millions of wonderful dogs like Freckles deserve a second chance at love and happiness with a family."

—BETTY WELTON, EXECUTIVE DIRECTOR
ARIZONA ANIMAL WELFARE LEAGUE
PHOENIX, ARIZONA

"… a compelling story of what it must feel like for a dog to be lost, trying to survive in the harsh desert environment. We learn about Freckles' courage in taking care of her young family and how those lessons contribute to her future work in helping kids as a therapy dog. Readers will be inspired to help other stray dogs who are also looking for loving homes."

—FAITH MALONEY, DIRECTOR
BEST FRIEND'S ANIMAL SANCTUARY
KANAB, UTAH

"I found reading *Freckles* to be a treat! It is that rare kind of book that appeals to both kids and adults with a message presented in such an intriguing and beguiling story."

—ROBERT H. GEORGE D.V.M., HEAD OF VETERINARY SERVICES
VIRGINIA MARINE SCIENCE MUSEUM
VIRGINIA BEACH, VA

"Paul Howey's book is a testimony to animal intelligence. Through Freckles' heroic behavior, she proves that animals can not only think and reason, but use their cognitive skills to protect the children they love. This is a delightful read for all ages. The courage and spirit of this brave little dog shine through every page!"

—AMELIA KINKADE, AUTHOR OF *STRAIGHT FROM THE HORSE'S MOUTH: HOW TO TALK TO ANIMALS AND GET ANSWERS*
NORTH HOLLYWOOD, CALIFORNIA

"I like Freckles because she listens to me."

—"ANDY" (AGE 8)
ONE OF FRECKLES' SPECIAL FRIENDS

FRECKLES

The Mystery of the Little White Dog in the Desert

A true story by

PAUL M. HOWEY

♦

Illustrations by JUDY MEHN ZABRISKIE

AZTexts Publishing, Inc.

Published by AZTexts Publishing, Inc.

AZTexts Publishing, Inc.
P.O. Box 93487
Phoenix, AZ 85070-3487
www.aztexts.com

First Edition

Publisher's Cataloging-in-Publication Data

Howey, Paul.
   Freckles : The mystery of the little white dog in the desert : a true story / by Paul M. Howey ; illustrations by Judy Mehn Zabriskie -- 1st ed.
     p. cm.
   SUMMARY: True story of an abandoned dog that's rescued from the desert and becomes a therapy dog working with homeless, abused and otherwise at-risk children.
   Audience: Ages 5-11
   LCCN 2002092171
   ISBN 0-9677292-1-1

1. Dogs--Juvenile literature. 2. Dog adoption-- Juvenile literature. 3. Dogs--Therapeutic use--Juvenile Literature. 4. Dogs--Training--Juvenile literature. [1. Dog adoption. 2. Dogs--Training. 3. Human-animal relationships.] I. Illustrator Judy Mehn Zabriskie. II. Title.

SF426.5.H69 2002   636.7'0887   QBI02-701627

EDITOR
Conrad J. Storad

BOOK DESIGN
Barbara Kordesh

BOOK PRODUCTION
Five Star Publications, Inc.

To my wife Trish
for knowing instinctively that Freckles
should be part of our family

ACKNOWLEDGMENTS

A special note of gratitude to Lt. Dave Williams of the Maricopa County Sheriff's Department and his colleague, Officer Kim Scarborough, who work tirelessly on behalf of animals. Dave rescued Freckles from the desert and Kim supervised the inmates who cared for Freckles and her pups. Together, their efforts make the world a better place for animals and for people.

A very large thank you to Conrad J. Storad for his expert editorial guidance. Conrad is the editor of the award-winning Arizona State University *Research Magazine* and the founding editor of *Chain Reaction*, a science magazine for young readers. He is also the author of many best-selling science and nature books for children and young adults.

It was a chance encounter with a pencil sketch of a baby orangutan that led me to one of the world's most gifted wildlife artists. Shortly after I told her about Freckles, Judy Mehn Zabriskie shared a nearly identical story about a dog and her puppies that she had rescued many years ago in Alaska. That was just the beginning of the many connections that we ultimately discovered in our lives. I will be forever grateful for the creative energy and enthusiasm and incredible talent that Judy poured into illustrating this book.

Thanks also to Linda Radke and Barbara Kordesh who instantly understood my vision for this book and helped bring it into reality with their unbeatable skills at layout and design.

The coyote was only a few feet away and getting closer. The little white dog was terrified. But she knew she had to protect her newborn puppies. She waited for just the right moment. Then she ran from her hiding place in the rocks and lunged at the coyote.

Barking and snarling, the little white dog bit the coyote's neck. Startled, the coyote jerked its head and flipped the little white dog end over end across the desert floor. The coyote spun around and then pounced, closing its jaws tightly about the dog's head.

The little white dog fought as hard as she could. She finally broke free and attacked the coyote again. That was enough for the coyote. It turned and ran away. The little white dog limped back to her puppies and laid down next to them. They were safe again, at least for a little while.

The Dog in the Desert

How the little white dog with brown spots ended up in the Sonoran Desert of southern Arizona is a mystery. But sometimes there are clues that can help you solve a mystery.

We don't know where the dog came from. Maybe someone didn't want her anymore. It's sad, but it happens sometimes. People often don't realize that taking care of a dog is a lot of work. Of course, they're excited about getting a new puppy. But then maybe the puppy chews a shoe or a pillow. That might make the people angry with the puppy. After a while, they may decide they don't want the puppy anymore.

If that's what happened to the little white dog, maybe she got scared and ran away. Or maybe her owner took her out in the desert and left her there. Anyway, that's where she was—frightened, confused, and very lonely.

Some time after she was stranded in the desert, the little white dog gave birth to six puppies. There were lots of things she had to do to keep her puppies safe.

The desert can be a very hot place. She had to find shade for herself and for her puppies. She also had to protect them from hungry animals that live in the desert—animals such as coyotes, who look something like dogs themselves.

Perhaps this is one of the clues.

If you look closely, you'll see what appear to be bite marks on the little white dog's head. Did she get these while fighting off a coyote or some other animal that wanted to get to her puppies? It's possible.

Lots of other creatures live in the desert. She had to keep her puppies safe from rattlesnakes and from hungry hawks that soar high above the desert floor, their keen eyes watching for mice and rabbits and other small animals.

She must have spent a lot of time day and night staying alert for animals that could hurt her puppies.

She had to find food to eat and water to drink, too.

How she managed to do some of these things will always remain a mystery.

We do know one thing. When the little white dog was rescued, she and her puppies were tired and skinny, but they were healthy and alive. She'd done a great job of caring for her little ones.

The Rescue

One day, Dave got a phone call. Dave is a deputy sheriff who makes sure animals are safe and well cared for. The caller said a white dog was running loose in the desert south of town. Dave reached for his jacket and his two-way radio and headed for his truck.

He drove way out in the desert, miles from the nearest house. He parked his truck and began walking, his eyes searching for any sign of the dog.

A cactus wren spotted him and sounded a warning from its perch atop a tall saguaro. Dave glanced up and smiled as he watched the little bird dart inside the nest it had built in one of the arms of the cactus. He continued on his way, careful to avoid the sharp spines of the cholla and prickly pear and other cactus.

Then he thought he saw a dog watching him from a nearby hilltop. He grabbed the trunk of a gnarled old mesquite tree to help him climb up the loose gravel slope. When he got to the top of the hill, however, the dog was nowhere to be seen.

"Now where did that rascal go?" muttered Dave. He sat down and leaned against a giant boulder. A Red-tailed hawk circled slowly in the late afternoon sky. Dave watched the graceful bird as it seemed to float effortlessly on the last warm air currents of the afternoon.

Then he heard something—a little yip and then a rustling noise. Dave looked all around but didn't see anything. He stood up and made his way cautiously to the other side of the boulder.

There, nestled deep in the rocks, was the little white dog with brown spots. The little white dog and one…two…three…four…five…six tiny puppies.

"Why, they can't be more than a few weeks old at most!" exclaimed Dave.

He stood still, not wanting to scare them. Dave reached into his pocket and pulled out some dog treats that he always carried.

"Here's something good to eat, little girl. I'll bet you and your pups are starving. How long have you been out here?"

Dave leaned down and offered a treat on his outstretched hand. The little white dog's eyes widened, but she didn't budge.

"You're pretty scared, aren't you? I would be, too. Besides, your mom probably told you never to take treats from a stranger. That's good advice."

Dave kept talking in a soft, soothing voice. He tossed the treat in her direction and it landed at her feet. She sniffed at it and then gobbled it up. When Dave held out another treat, the little dog began inching toward him.

When she got close enough, Dave slipped a collar over her

head and snapped on a leash. She was terrified. She thrashed and pulled and bit at the leash, trying desperately to get away.

"Calm down now, little girl. I'm not going to hurt you. I just want to help you and your little ones."

Dave quickly scooped up the puppies and put them in the big side pockets of his jacket. Then he started the long walk back to his truck. The little white dog came along, too. Dave didn't even have to pull on the leash. This strange man had her puppies wriggling and squealing in his pockets. She had no choice but to go with him.

Dave opened up the back of his truck and placed the little white dog inside a kennel. He rummaged around and found an old blanket and put it next to her. Then he reached into his pockets and carefully pulled out each of the puppies and laid them on the blanket next to their mother.

When they were all safe and secure, Dave drove back to his office at the county jail.

The Dogs Go to Jail

What a shock! Just a few hours earlier, they had been running loose in the desert. Now here they were, soaking wet from being scrubbed down and sitting on the floor of the county jail.

What would happen to the little white dog and her puppies now that they were in jail?

They didn't have to worry. The people who ran the jail loved animals.

The little white dog and her puppies would stay there until new homes could be found for them. Three women at the jail were put in charge of taking care of them. The women fed them, bathed them, brushed them, and played with them. After a few weeks, the puppies were old enough to be adopted.

Adoption Day

This is the day people would visit the jail and see if they wanted to adopt any of the dogs. The three women got up early. They wanted to make sure the little white dog and her puppies were all cleaned up and looking their very best.

They were excited for the dog and her puppies to find new homes. But they were sad, too. They knew they were going to miss all the love their furry, warm companions had brought into their lives.

Meanwhile, across town, a woman was reading the morning newspaper when she spotted an article describing the "adoption day" at the county jail.

"This sounds like a wonderful program," the woman said

after reading the story to her husband. "You know how much we love our animals and how much joy they bring us. I'll bet the people in that jail are learning a lot from the dogs."

Then she said, "I'd like to go down there. Maybe there's some way I could help out." She saw the look on her husband's face and quickly added, "But don't worry. I won't adopt any of the dogs."

"I'm glad to hear that," the man answered with a laugh. "The three dogs we have now keep us plenty busy!"

That night when the man got home, his wife met him at the door.

"Honey," she said, "I think we have a project in the back-yard."

"Oh, no," the man said. "That old gate didn't break again, did it?"

She didn't say a word. Instead, she just led him by the hand through the house. When they got to the patio door, she stopped.

"What have you done?" the man gasped. On the other side of the sliding glass door was a little white dog looking back at him.

"Well…I…uh….I…"

"You adopted this dog down at the jail, didn't you?" her husband asked. He wasn't exactly smiling.

"Well, yes. I just wanted to check out the program. I certainly didn't plan on adopting any of the dogs but…"

She paused and smiled weakly at her husband. She motioned for him to follow her outside to the patio where the little white dog sat, her ears flat against her head, her tail between her legs.

"Hi there, little fella," the man said.

"She," the woman corrected.

"What?"

"It's a girl."

The woman described how the dog and her puppies had been rescued from the desert. She told her husband that all of the puppies had been adopted right away but that nobody wanted the little white dog.

"She was frightened and hiding under one of the cots in the cell," the woman said. "She probably had no idea what was happening or where her puppies had gone."

The man called to the little white dog, but she just whimpered and backed away from him.

"Anyhow, I sat down on the floor of the jail cell," the woman continued. "At first, she'd only look at me for a second or two and then turn away. After a while though, I caught her staring at me. Before I knew it, she was sitting next to me."

The man tried again. "Come here, girl," he said quietly to the little dog, offering the back of his hand for her to sniff. She cringed and let out a little whine. He took another step toward her. This time, she ran away from him and hid behind a tree.

She acts like somebody used to hit her, he thought. The man couldn't understand why anyone would hurt a dog. He knew how special all creatures are, especially dogs who only want to love you and make you happy.

The woman continued, "And since the 'adoption day' was almost over, I decided to bring her home with me." She stopped to see what her husband's reaction might be.

"Oh, so you didn't adopt her? You just brought her home for the night?"

"Well…"

"You did," the man said. "You adopted her without asking me, didn't you?"

The woman nodded.

"But four dogs is too many!" he exclaimed. "She's a sweet dog, but you'll have to take her back. I can't believe you brought home a dog without checking with me first."

"You're right," the woman admitted. "I shouldn't have done that. I promise I'll find her a new home tomorrow." Then she added, "I'm going to the store. I'll only be gone a few minutes. As soon as I get back, I'll make some phone calls."

When she got home, she looked all through the house, but she couldn't find her husband anywhere. She went out to the patio and turned on the yard light. There he was, sitting in the middle of the lawn next to the little white dog with brown spots.

"Hi, honey," he said cheerfully. "I'd like you to meet Freckles."

"Freckles? You've named her? Why on earth would you do that if we're going to find her a new home?"

"Find her a new home? This is our dog you're talking about. She's not going anywhere!"

"You mean we can keep her?" the woman shouted.

"Of course, we're keeping her. That was pretty sneaky, leaving me alone with her while you went to the store. You knew I'd fall in love with her right away, didn't you?"

"Me?" she laughed. "Would I do something like that?"

The man got up and opened the door. The couple's other three dogs ran out and joined them. They all sniffed at the little white dog. They wagged their tails and romped around the yard trying to get her to play with them.

Freckles was home at last.

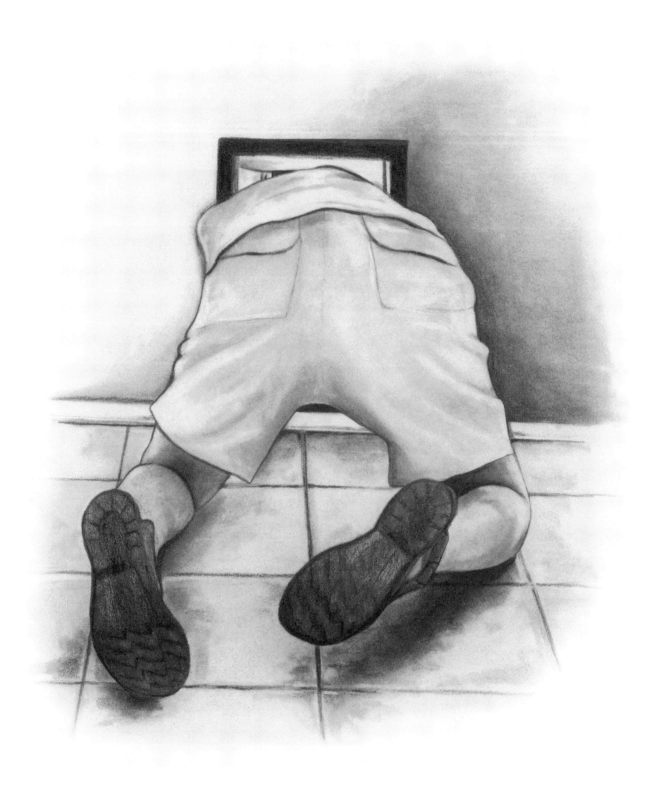

Fitting In

It's not easy being the new dog.

Have you ever moved to a new neighborhood or gone to a new school? Were you a little scared or perhaps sad at first? Did it seem like the other kids already had friends and there was no way they'd ever want to make room for you?

That must have been how Freckles felt. She must have thought the other dogs in the family didn't want her butting in. So she didn't. She just stayed by herself. Most of the time, she hid in the backyard where no one could find her.

Slowly, the man and the woman were able to coax her out of her hiding places. But there was still a lot of work to do.

They enrolled Freckles in an obedience school. The man and

woman knew how important it is for all dogs to be trained. It makes them nicer to be around and can help keep them safe, too. So Freckles went to obedience school. Over the next several weeks, she was taught all of the basic commands.

Freckles was a very smart dog and learned things quickly. There was the doggie door, for example.

The man and woman had put in a little door so their dogs could go out to the backyard whenever they wanted to. Freckles had never seen such a thing. It took a lot of coaxing to get her to use it. In fact, the man nearly got stuck in the doggie door trying to show Freckles how it worked.

All in all, everything went very smoothly. In fact, Freckles and the other dogs were soon taking naps together all curled up on a blanket.

Some More Clues

The man and woman were amazed by some of the things Freckles did.

One time, while they were walking all four dogs, their beagle suddenly began barking at a neighbor's dog that was behind a fence. Freckles spun around and ran at the little beagle. She took the back of his neck in her teeth, and shook him a couple of times.

"Did you see that?" the man asked excitedly.

"I sure did," his wife answered. "What just happened?"

"You know how we said little Freckles is like a mystery with only a few clues to go on?"

"Are you saying this was some kind of clue?" she asked.

"Of course, I can't be sure," the man said. "But I'll bet she was trying to get our beagle to be quiet so he wouldn't draw attention to himself and maybe get hurt by that other dog."

"How is that supposed to be a clue?" his wife asked.

"Well, just imagine Freckles out in the desert with her puppies. She had to protect them from all kinds of animals."

He leaned down and petted each of the dogs. "What do you suppose she would have done if a hawk were circling overhead and one of her puppies began to bark?"

"She probably would have grabbed her puppy by the scruff of the neck and made it be quiet," the woman offered.

"Yes. A moment ago when our beagle barked, I think Freckles was still being a mother, trying to protect him from harm."

A few minutes later, they were out in the desert not far from their house. While the other dogs scurried around with their noses close to the ground, excited at all the new smells, Freckles stayed out in front. She kept her head up, her eyes constantly scanning the desert for anything that might be moving.

"Our city dogs have no idea what goes on in the desert," the woman said. "But Freckles is aware of everything out here. She's always taking care of the other dogs."

"Thanks for all the clues, Freckles!" the man said, rubbing the little dog gently behind the ears. "You're helping us to get to know you even better."

The next day, the man and the woman took their granddaughter for a walk in the nearby mountains that rise from the desert floor. It was a beautiful, warm morning—a perfect day for being outdoors. They brought Freckles with them.

They were hiking along the trail when the little girl let go of her grandmother's hand and skipped ahead along the narrow path.

"Come back here, honey," the woman said. "It's not safe for you to walk by yourself. See how far down it is?"

The little girl stopped and looked over the edge. It was a long way down. But she wasn't scared. She started skipping again.

Freckles saw what was happening and ran

after the little girl. When she caught up with her, Freckles stood between her and the edge of the trail so the little girl couldn't move.

When the woman got there, she swooped her granddaughter into her arms and held her tightly. "Thank goodness, you're okay!"

She looked at her husband. "Did you see what Freckles just did?"

The man stood there shaking his head. "If I hadn't seen it, I wouldn't have believed it. Not only does Freckles protect our other dogs, she watches over our granddaughter, too."

"I think Freckles is very special," the woman said.

A Special Job for Freckles

Look at this story on pet therapy," the woman said as she slid the magazine across the table to her husband. "It's about dogs helping children."

The man glanced at the article. "That's really nothing new, is it?" he asked. "They've used dogs and other animals for years to comfort and cheer up hospital patients and elderly people."

"I know," his wife answered, "but these people and their dogs work only with children.

A lot of these kids love animals but aren't allowed to have pets where they live. Some of them might have had a rough start in life, too. It may be they don't have a home right now. The important thing is the therapy dogs love these kids no matter who they are or what they've been through."

The man looked at his wife.

"Are you thinking what I'm thinking?" she asked him.

"What? That maybe Freckles would make a good therapy dog?" he asked with a chuckle.

She smiled back at him. "As a matter of fact, that's exactly what I'm thinking. We know how she is with our other dogs and with our granddaughter, too. She's very protective and caring. It's as though she has a special sense about things."

They decided to find out more.

They met with the people from the pet therapy group. The people loved Freckles. They said Freckles was intelligent and gentle and might be a perfect therapy dog.

But first, there had to be more training. It was important for Freckles to learn how to be relaxed in a variety of new and different situations and around strangers, too. After several weeks, Freckles was ready to take the test to become a pet therapy dog. She passed!

Freckles had a job, a very important job. She was going to work with kids.

Freckles' first assignment was to visit a special nursery that cared for very young children. All of the kids were excited to meet her. All of them except one.

One little boy didn't come up to pet Freckles. In fact, Tony spent the entire time sitting under a table all by himself. The woman in charge of the nursery said he was always like that.

"Tony's only been here a few days," she explained, "but he hasn't said a word to any of us yet."

Freckles played and played with the other children. She sat still while they took turns brushing her soft, white fur. After a while, the children left one by one to go play with the toys that were in the room.

When she was all alone, Freckles got up and went over to the table where Tony was hiding. She spent the rest of the visit just lying there a few feet from him.

The next week when Freckles went back to the nursery, it happened again. The children played with Freckles and petted her and brushed her coat. Then they took turns walking her around the room. When they were all done, Freckles went over to the table and laid down next to Tony.

The third week was just the same. Except this time when Freckles went over to Tony, he reached out and petted her on the back. When he did this, Freckles slowly moved closer to him. Nobody could hear what he was saying. But anyone watching could see he was talking to Freckles. Freckles stayed next to him, her head resting in his lap.

On the fourth visit, Tony ran to the door with the other children to greet Freckles when she arrived.

"That's absolutely amazing," said the woman who ran the nursery. "All these weeks, none of us has been able to get Tony to talk. And who got him to talk? A dog! A wonderful, loving dog." She reached down and gave Freckles a great big hug.

Before she left the nursery that day, Freckles looked around the room at all the children. While we may never know everything about Freckles, there was certainly no mystery about the way the little white dog from the desert felt.

As she stood there slowly wagging her tail, her soft eyes seemed to say to each child, "I understand. I really do."

Freckles loves children of all ages. She now visits every week with a group of teenage girls who call her their girlfriend. Freckles even got them to go hiking with her in the nearby mountains where she made certain they didn't get too close to the edge!

Here's some great information for kids who want to know more!

(and for parents, teachers, and other adults, too)

Glossary

Sonoran (suh–NOR–un) Desert   Freckles' story begins in the Sonoran Desert. The Sonoran Desert is an arid (it receives only 4 to 12 inches—100 to 300 millimeters—of rain each year) region. It covers more than 120,000 square miles (324,000 square kilometers) in southwestern Arizona, southeastern California, and extending southward into Mexico. While some deserts of the world are vast expanses of sand dunes, the Sonoran Desert is known for its rock features and mountains and the wide variety of animals and plants that live there. Daytime temperatures in the summer in the Sonoran Desert are frequently over 100 degrees Fahrenheit (38 degrees Celsius), and often as high as 115 degrees (46 degrees Celsius) or more.

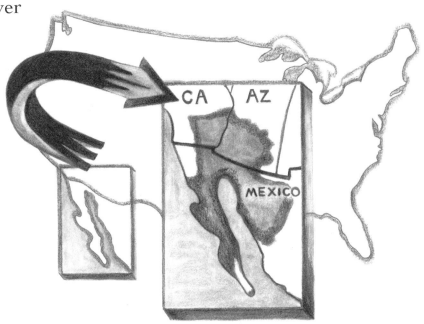

HERE'S INFORMATION ABOUT SOME OF THE WORDS YOU READ
IN THIS STORY:

cactus wren   The state bird of
Arizona, the cactus wren builds
its nests in cholla and other large,
thorny plants. It also builds nests
in holes made by woodpeckers in saguaro
cactus. Cactus wrens eat insects such as
ants, beetles, and grasshoppers. They also eat
fruits and seeds and occasionally small frogs and lizards.

cholla (CHOY–yuh)   There are
several different kinds of cholla cactus that live in the Sonoran Desert.
Cholla are made up of spine-covered
cylinders all connected together. These
segments are designed to break off easi-
ly when touched. In fact, they come off
so quickly that one type is known as the Jumping Cholla!

coyote (kye–YO–tee) Coyotes are slender, gray/brown animals that are related to (but smaller than) wolves. Coyotes are found in Alaska, throughout Canada and much of the United States, and south through Mexico and Central America. Their diet consists mainly of small mammals, but they also eat fruits, insects, frogs, and snakes.

hawk There are several different types of hawks that live in the Sonoran Desert. One of the most common is the Red-tailed hawk. It is one of the largest of all hawks. It has a wingspan of more than 4 feet (1.2 meters) and weighs between 2 and 4 pounds (.9 to 1.8 kilograms). The eyesight of the Red-tailed hawk is at least 8 times more powerful than that of humans. Red-tailed hawks feed primarily on small rodents and snakes, often spotting them while soaring hundreds of feet above the desert floor.

mesquite (MESS–keet) The mesquite is a thorny tree that grows in warm places throughout the southwestern United States and into Mexico. It thrives in the dry stream beds of the Sonoran Desert. Mesquite trees grow to an average height of 20 to 30 feet (6 to 9 meters). The mesquite has greenish white flowers and its seed pods are eaten by many different animals.

prickly pear (PRICK–lee pare) Prickly pear cactus grow in nearly every state in the United States (except Maine, Vermont, and New Hampshire). Prickly pear cactus are made up of flat, fleshy pads joined together.

rattlesnakes There are 17 different types of rattlesnakes that call the Sonoran Desert home. Of these, the most common is the Western Diamondback rattlesnake. The Western Diamondback

can grow to a length of 5 to 6
feet (1.5 to 1.8 meters). Its
rattle is a horny section at
the end of its tail that it
shakes to scare off potential
attackers. The Western
Diamondback's diet consists

primarily of small rodents, rabbits, birds, and other small animals.
It is one of the most dangerous snakes in the United States.

saguaro (suh–WAHR–oh)   The saguaro cactus is the giant of
the Sonoran Desert, the only place in the world where it lives.
Extremely slow-growing, a saguaro cactus
may be only 6 feet (1.8 meters) tall on
its 50th birthday. By the time it's 75 to
100 years old, it will begin to grow its
familiar arms. Saguaros can live to be
200 years old or more, growing as
high as 40 to 50 feet (12 to 15
meters) and weighing as much as 8
tons (7.25 metric tons). The fragrant
white blossom of the saguaro is the
state flower of Arizona.

10 Things to Talk About

Freckles' story touches on many different topics. Here are a few questions about some of them. Use these questions to talk about this story with others.

1. Why was Freckles in the desert?

2. What things do puppies do that might make someone angry or upset?

3. Freckles had to protect herself and her puppies from some of the animals that live in the desert. Can you name some of these animals?

4. Why were Freckles' puppies adopted right away but no one seemed to want her?

5. Where are some places you can get a dog?

6. When Freckles was adopted, why did she seem to be scared of the man?

7. Can you think of some reasons why it's important to train your dog?

8. What are some other things you need to do if you have a dog?

9. What are pet therapy animals and why do you think Freckles is such a good pet therapy dog?

10. Why is it important to be kind to dogs and other animals?

SOME THOUGHTS ABOUT
ADOPTING A DOG

Most dogs live 10 to 15 years or more. When you bring an animal into your family, you need to know that it's a lifetime commitment. Be absolutely certain you're willing to spend the necessary time and money before getting a dog. It's one of the most important decisions you will ever make.

Do your research. Dogs come in all sizes and temperaments and needs. Select the one that matches your home and family environment. Freckles was rescued from the desert and eventually found a permanent and loving home. Most abandoned animals, however, are not nearly as fortunate. Tragically, more than half of all stray cats and dogs are euthanized simply because no one claims them or adopts them.

When you're ready to get a dog, please consider adopting your pet from an animal shelter. You'll be saving a life. How often do you have the opportunity to do something that wonderful?

Also, please consider adopting an older dog. There's no denying that puppies are cute (they almost always get adopted quickly), but older dogs are also special. Besides, it's possible you may get to skip the chewing and house-training stages. If you do get a puppy, make sure you give it plenty of toys to play with and to chew (remember, all puppies like to chew).

Dogs are the essence of unconditional love and acceptance. Please don't abuse this gift. Love your animals. Play with your animals. Be patient with your animals. Train your animals (behavior problems are the reasons most people give when turning in pets at an animal shelter). License your animals. Never let your animals run loose (not only is it against the law in most places, it often leads to tragic consequences). Spay or neuter your animals (pet overpopulation is a huge problem).

Finally, whether you have pets in your family or not, please support the animal shelters in your community. They could really use your contributions of money and time. You'll like the people you meet there, too. They are among the nicest and most caring folks you'll ever encounter.

MORE ABOUT PET THERAPY

Freckles is part of a growing number of dogs and other pets whose owners volunteer their time in hopes of making a difference in the lives of others. Dogs, cats, gerbils, rabbits, birds, horses, and many other animals are being used to help people in hospitals, elderly people, children, and people with physical and emotional problems.

So what is it that the animals do? Quite simply, be themselves. The simple act of holding an animal in your lap and stroking its fur can make you feel better. Pets are great listeners, too. They never talk back or tell you that you're wrong. They can even make you smile and laugh sometimes when you're feeling sad. Importantly, many animals can sense when you're hurting or upset. They often just curl up next to you to let you know that they're there, that they love you, that they would do anything to make you feel better. What more could anyone ask?

Sadly, many children who are in an abusive environment grow up to become abusive adults or become trapped in abusive relationships. Pet-assisted therapy can do much to break this cycle of violence by helping children establish healthy, nurturing, and long-lasting relationships with other living creatures.

"Our pet therapy teams offer unconditional love, teach respect, empathy, and trust," says Pam Gaber, founder of Gabriel's Angels, the group Freckles volunteers with. "The power of these therapy dogs is amazing. They have an uncanny way of helping the children cope with the turmoil in their lives."

If you're interested in learning more, check with your local library. You can also place the phrase "animal-assisted therapy" or "pet therapy" in a search engine and see all the websites on the subject that the Internet has to offer. For more information about what it takes to become involved in animal-assisted therapy, check out the Delta Society (www.DeltaSociety.org).

ABOUT THE AUTHOR
Paul M. Howey

Paul is a member of the Society of Children's Book Writers and Illustrators and has written and edited several books for young readers as well as for adults. He volunteers for several animal-related organizations and teaches humane education classes at Boys and Girls Clubs.

He and his wife Trish live in Phoenix, Arizona. In addition to Freckles and their other dogs, they share their home with parrots, tortoises, and have a pond full of those large, colorful fish called Japanese koi. Anybody who visits their house had better like animals!

"I can't imagine my life without being surrounded by animals," says Paul. "They have so much to teach us."

Freckles and Trish are a trained Pet Partners therapy team certified by the Delta Society and are volunteers with Gabriel's Angels, a Phoenix-based organization. Because of her story of survival and service, Freckles was named "Pet of the Year" by the Arizona Animal Welfare League.

Twenty percent of all proceeds from this book will go into a special Freckles Friends fund that will benefit animal rescue and animal-assisted therapy organizations. If you'd like more information about Freckles, adopting animals, or about pet therapy, please visit **www.FrecklesFriends.org**, or write:

Freckles Friends™
c/o AZTexts Publishing, Inc.
P.O. Box 93487
Phoenix, AZ 85070-3487

ABOUT THE ILLUSTRATOR
Judy Mehn Zabriskie

Judy was born and raised in the Chicago area and has lived in Missouri, Utah, Alaska, Florida, and Washington. A graduate of the University of Utah with a bachelor's degree in fine art with an emphasis in drawing and painting, her work is in public and private collections throughout the United States and in England, Costa Rica, Canada, Africa, and Australia. She is the education director for Las Baulas Leatherback Sea Turtle Project in Guanacaste, Costa Rica, and also volunteers her time on behalf of Books Without Boundaries and children's peace organizations.

She and her husband and son live in Monona, Wisconsin, along with their dog, two cats, and four box turtles. "In addition to my family and animals, my greatest passions," says Judy, "are drawing and interacting with children."

Her work as a wildlife artist and as an educator have made her a strong believer in conservation and in the preservation of all species. Judy says she was so moved by Freckles' story that she adopted a second dog from an animal rescue organization. She has enrolled both of her dogs in training classes which she hopes will lead them to becoming therapy dogs.